9849

917.43

D1591857

Vermont

Vermont
in all weathers

Photographs by
Sonja Bullaty and Angelo Lomeo

Text by Noel Perrin

A Studio Book
THE VIKING PRESS
New York

Contents

to Nicolas Ducrot who made this book possible
Sonja Bullaty and
Angelo Lomeo

for Linda,
whose one fault is that she lives in New Hampshire
Noel Perrin

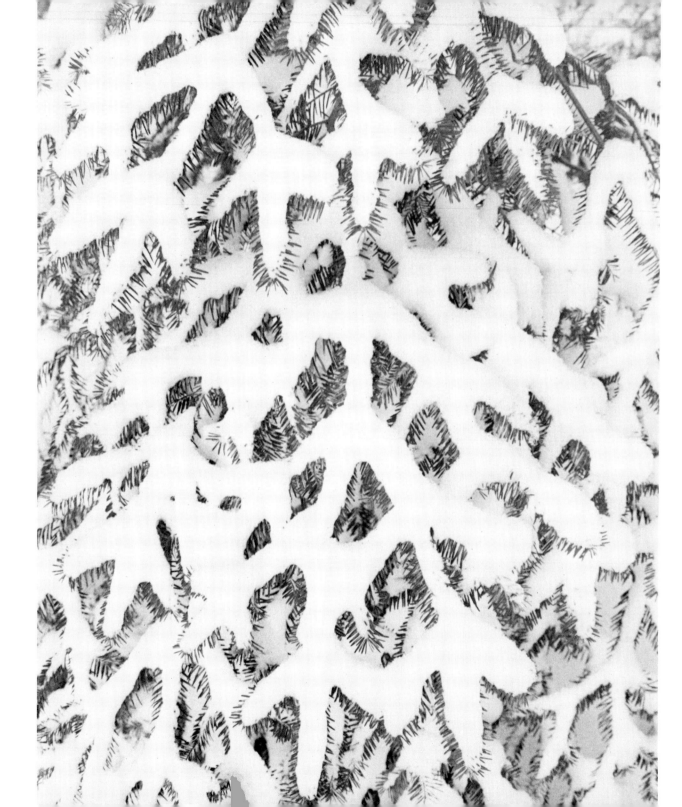

Foreword

There are three things everybody knows about Vermont, and two of them are false. Everybody knows that Vermont is (1) the state where cows outnumber people, (2) the place maple syrup comes from, and (3) unspoiled.

The second of these statements is true. Vermont is indeed the place maple syrup comes from. It comes from other places, too—and not only the ones you'd expect, like New Hampshire and Canada. There is a little produced as far south as Virginia, and quite a lot as far west as Michigan. Pennsylvania is a big maple syrup state, and New York a bigger one. But Vermonters make the most maple syrup (some years in absolute terms, every year per capita), and the best. They also have the best-looking sugarhouses.

As for cows outnumbering people, that charming statistic held true for more than a century. Cows moved ahead in 1850, and stayed ahead until 1965. At some unknown point that year men caught up again, and the two species came into balance: 395,000 Vermonters, 395,000 cows. Just about the right number of each, in my opinion. It didn't last. Since then, cows have gone slowly down, and people relentlessly up. There are now nearly 450,000 Vermonters, and only 351,000 cows. This has been bad for pastures.

The third statement was true from the end of the last ice age until about 1970. It is still partly true. As the pictures in this book show, Vermont still has its wooded hills, its wild-flowered meadows, its tranquil farms, its stunning views. It is still a kind of rural backwater in the otherwise bulging Northeast, a state in which the largest city has 38,000 people—and one of the other seven cities has 2242.

But the pictures don't show everything. They don't show the numerous and growing trailer parks, the even more numerous real-estate developments. They don't show the Boston-based land investment firms, the realty offices in places like Greenwich, Connecticut, devoted solely to buying and selling of Vermont land. Very often to the dismemberment of Vermont farms. The number of spoilers at work is large.

Vermont's climate, its topography, and not least its legislature will protect the state from utter spoliation. I have every faith that a century from now there will be farmers with woodburning stoves, and perhaps there will even be dirt roads. The hills are not going to go away, either. Nor the sugar maples. (This past spring was very wet, hence favorable to germination; and two or three hundred seeded themselves in my barnyard alone.) The number of covered bridges is actually rising now, after a fifty-year decline.

But there is already one town in the state that is about as unspoiled as Jersey City. It will take more than our long winters and the present enlightened but mild legislation being passed to save some of the others. Most of all, it will take new tax laws and new laws on land speculation. Land speculation is, I admit, traditional in the state. Ethan and Ira Allen were both big speculators, and they were not the first. But eighteenth-century speculation was different. For example, when an ambitious speculator like Thomas Brantingham of New York City bought sixteen thousand acres of Vermont land in 1792, he in no way inconvenienced the trout or the bears, much less brought in a series of burger stands. Even if Brantingham had succeeded in developing the land, it would simply have become about a hundred Vermont farms—fewer bears, in that case, but more cows.

The great corporate developers now are less beneficial. The sale of sixteen thousand acres is likely to mean sixteen thousand ski chalets, two golf courses, a bowling alley, another denuded mountain, a shopping center, and a further small decline in cows and maple syrup.

Come to Vermont, by all means. But come to lead the life of the state, not to spoil it. And what is that life? Some aspects of it, as people and other creatures live it month by month throughout the year, appear in the following pages. If weather seems predominant, that's because it is so in the state itself.

Noel Perrin
Thetford Center, Vermont

January

During three months in the year, this part of America is covered with snow.

—The Rev. Dr. Samuel Williams, *The Natural and Civil History of Vermont,* 1794

Either the climate has changed a lot in the last hundred and eighty years, or Dr. Williams was an incorrigible optimist. Four and a half months is more like it, and sometimes it's five. There is an awful lot of snow. The winter of 1971–1972, for example, started with a blizzard on November 25. We had a white Thanksgiving, marked by many missing guests. Then a white Christmas, a white Valentine's Day, and a white Easter. The snow was just beginning to go from the fields—not yet from the woods—the week after Easter, when another big storm came sliding in. It restored a foot of snow to open ground and built the level in the woods back up to three feet. I got my truck stuck in a snowdrift on April 14. There was no bare ground worth mentioning until April 20. Five full months winter lasted.

Of all this time, January is the supreme snow month. I'm not saying the most snow falls then, because it doesn't. In January it's usually too cold to snow as much as it does in, say, March. But the snow and the biting cold dominate life in a way they do at no other time.

They even dominate aesthetically. January is the month of blue shadows. Whether it's the lowness of the sun, or the absolute purity of the air, the unsullied whiteness of the snow, or merely some kind of reflection from the bright January sky, I have no idea. But in January when the sun puts the shadow of a line of trees across a snowy field, the shadow is a blue-gray to be seen in no other circumstances. It is almost worth being that cold to snowshoe or ski-tour out to look at shadows. Late afternoon—that is, three to four o'clock; it's going to be dark before five—is the best time.

Except for shadow-watching, there are fairly few outdoor amusements in Vermont in January. Downhill skiers are out, and snowmobilers go snowmobiling, usually in small herds of about a dozen. You often hear them at bedtime. (Like deer and rabbits, snowmobilers are mainly nocturnal; and like other native species they have developed a special winter coat that keeps them warm on even the coldest nights.) Small children occasionally get a certain pleasure out of squeaking. This they can do simply by walking around outside any time the temperature drops to ten above or colder. The snow squeaks at each step.

Grown-ups occasionally get a certain pleasure out of splitting elm logs, especially if they have previously tried splitting them in the summer. Elm is a cross-grained wood, and most of the year a big elm log is hard or even impossible to split in two. You have to keep working around the perimeter, like a veneer machine, or one person making a double bed. But now the sap is frozen, and one well-placed blow in the heartwood will often cause even quite large elm logs to shiver apart. Better use a good splitting maul, though. When it's that cold, badly tempered steel sometimes shivers, too.

Most Januaries there is a period of five or ten days when nonstop squeaking would be possible and when everything shivers. The temperature drops to fifteen or twenty below every night and climbs to perhaps two above at the warmest instant of the day. If there is also a wind blowing, anyone except a snowmobiler in his special suit or a fanatic skier wearing a face mask can comfortably be outdoors for approximately ten minutes. Hairy and downy woodpeckers, who have to be out all the time, need special attention now. Frozen grubs just won't keep them going; they crave an Eskimo diet. I have seen a handful of small woodpeckers go through a pound of pork fat in one day.

Machinery is also hard to keep going, and a large number of decisions to buy a new car is made annually during this period. The first morning that your car won't start, you are angry. The second, you are furious. Also late to work, since the man who owns the garage has eight other cars to start before he can get to yours. That night you decide to take your battery out and keep it in the house until morning. But your hands get so cold trying to loosen the terminals that you compromise by leaving it in the car and putting an old blanket over the hood. You also go out at bedtime and let the engine run for twenty minutes. When it doesn't start the third morning, you are fair game for Detroit.

For the handful of Vermonters who still keep driving horses, however, the January cold spell is a moment of glory. A neighbor of mine is fond of telling of a January morning that was cold even beyond the usual for cold spells. Along with a crowd of other men, he was down at Varney's Store in South Strafford, waiting to use the tractor starter. While he was waiting, an old fellow came driving up in a horse and buggy, looking insufferably smug. (He can't use his sleigh since we started salting the roads.)

"I knowed him," my neighbor says, "so I said, "Morning, Earl! How cold was it up to your place?'" The old fellow gave his horse a flick. "Dunno. Thermometer only goes down to minus forty." He looked the crowd of men over carelessly and added, "Hoss don't care, anyway."

I myself knew a Vermont girl of twenty who did housecleaning and baby-sitting one winter for the family of a Dartmouth professor. It gets just as cold across the river in New Hampshire. Doreen had a fifteen-year-old Dodge she drove to work. When she appeared right on time the fourth morning in a row of January cold spell—a morning, as it happens, that her employer was waiting impatiently for the garageman to come start his new Ford station wagon—he broke down and asked her what her trick was. No trick at all. "Daddy just hitches up the team," she said, "and drags me till it starts."

January is not all cold and snow. Along toward the end of the month comes a myth known as the January thaw. It is not entirely a myth, either. There was a period of three days in January 1964 when the temperature never went below freezing and it hardly ever stopped raining. On January 31, 1968, just before noon, the temperature on the front porch of my farmhouse went up to fifty-six. Later in the day I went up to thirty. Feet, that is. On a ladder. Onto the roof to chop ice. Once a foot or so of snow has built up on the roof of the house, it begins to melt a little on the underside, from the heat of the house. A little water trickles quietly down under the snow to the eaves, where it promptly freezes again. By the time of January thaw an ice dam six or eight inches high will have built up. What with the rain and the thawing weather, a good-sized lake now forms behind it. Presently a stream of water comes coursing down the wallpaper in the front hall. It is time to chop ice, and I do. Just for a minute I consider selling the farm as well as the car and moving to some place like Arizona.

February

*The severest cold of our winters never kills any of our young trees,
and seldom freezes any of our young cattle, although they are not
housed during the winter. Nor is the cold so affecting to the human
body, as the extremes and sudden changes from heat to cold on the
sea coast.*

—Samuel Williams, 1794

Considering that I have had two successive sets of young pear trees winter-
killed, I cannot wholly agree with this claim, either. (A third pair, from a different nursery, has survived nicely, and if all goes well I hope to harvest my
first eleven pears this fall.) But Dr. Williams is certainly right about cattle
and people. We get through winters fine. It may have been a little chilly during
the January cold spell, and if there was also a January thaw, the slush was
horrible. But the rest of winter is a pleasure, and especially February is.

In February the days are longer, the sun is higher, and the snow is more
dramatic. Sometimes it is downright stagy. An evening flurry will come down
in huge wet flakes, so thick and fast that you think in an hour the village will
be buried like Pompeii. But the flurry stops in ten minutes, leaving two inches
of perfect snowball snow, the first since Christmas. More often there will be
a drifting snow of big feathery flakes. Floating down at midnight past the
streetlight at the east end of the covered bridge in Thetford Center, the flakes
seem (1) something holy, and (2) too much and too beautiful, as if there were
a Broadway stage crew dropping them from a helicopter a hundred feet up.

The morning after such a snow is what gave rise to picture postcards in the
first place. The sky is clear. The air is still and cold, but not too cold. The snow
doesn't squeak. From every chimney in the village a thick plume of smoke is
rising straight upward. Every tree branch and even every strand of barbed wire
has its snow tracery. When you drive to work (your car roaring easily to life,
even though you didn't get a new one, after all), you pass through a little
valley with an unfrozen brook running through it. The brook is sending up so
much vapor into the fifteen-degree air that for fifty yards on either side the
branches, the barbed wire, the very weeds (where they are tall and come up
through the snow) are mere vehicles for crystals and complicated jewelry
of ice.

Later in the day it's likely to be good weather for children to make snowmen and snow forts. In January it was too cold, and the snow wouldn't pack. Now it gets above freezing for several hours most days. Occasionally there is even a day that stirs the trees. February 2, 1969, for example, was such a day in Thetford. I was putting up a new fence to make a pasture for the horse I intended to get come spring. No one sinks fence posts in February, and I was stringing wire along a section of old stone wall where I could be a sloven and fasten it to the trees.

About halfway I came to a fair-sized sugar maple. I had the wire pretty tight, and the first staple I tried to drive went part way in and then pulled out again. Immediately a gush of sap poured out the two little holes, as if the tree were bleeding from a snakebite. One could have made syrup that day.

By no means are all February days like that. On February 13, 1967, it was thirty-one below when I got up. The pipes in the kitchen were frozen solid, the pigs were buried under straw in their pighouse, and though they came charging out for breakfast, the last of their slops froze in the trough before they could gulp them down.

But mostly there is some mildness in the air. And because so much of Vermont is steep hillsides, the reviving sun is able to melt snow on south cants even while it remains three feet deep on level ground and four feet or more on northern slopes. My two beef cattle were able to do a little grazing around the bases of trees even on that day that started at thirty-one below. Seldom except during an actual blizzard do they even bother to go into the three-sided shelter (open to the south, of course) that I built just below the spring in their pasture. Just as Dr. Williams said.

I am out a good deal myself now. February days are wonderful for walking in the woods. I used to do it mostly on snowshoes, but since the advent of the snowmobile, I walk on snowmobile trails. Once this past winter I was following one up Jackson Brook and came on what I can only describe as a deer highway, crossing at right angles. It was a well-trodden path about eight inches wide (two-lane for deer). Even sharply marked by color, because so many beech and oak leaves had drifted into it. A tan-brown highway through the white snow. I turned right and followed it, and in about a mile came to a deeryard I had never known existed. Six deer were home when I got there—placid enough so that instead of exploding out in all directions when they smelled me, they left at a trot, single file on another highway at the far side.

I wish Interstates 89 and 91 left as little mark on Vermont as those two highways did when I went back to see them in May.

March

The weather is cold, and, in general, pretty uniformly so . . . until the beginning of March, when with much boisterous weather there begin to appear some slight indications of spring.
      —Zadock Thompson, *History of Vermont*, 1842

Slight indications indeed. They do not include green fields—the first small patches of green appear in pastures about mid-April—much less early flowers, or leaves on the trees. Both of those belong to May. In fact, spring is the wrong word altogether. As someone pointed out a few years ago, Vermont does not have four seasons but six. First comes unlocking, then spring, summer, fall, locking, and finally winter. What begins in March is unlocking. Its enemies call it mud season, because what unlocks first is the ground, but that's not a fair name. There *is* considerable mud, but there is also much beauty of kinds never to be seen in warmer or drier climates.

Just as unlocking begins, there is one indication, so subtle and slight that it's easily missed. Every year some one of the first four or five days in March is going to be warm and brilliantly sunny, with the temperature briefly rising to somewhere between fifty and sixty. If you look hard at a birch or a red maple that day, you seem to see a faint haze of color in the upper branches: yellow for a birch, and red, of course for a red maple. Look again the next day, and it's gone. Nothing but bare dark branches, and probably a sleet storm. All the same, unlocking has begun.

Dirt roads unlock first, being the only ground not covered by snow. Each warm day the top inch or two of road touched by the sun thaws out. The first car going by makes a couple of inch-deep ruts, which get frozen in that evening. The next warm day they thaw and, with the first car, deepen, until presently only four-wheel-drive vehicles, and sometimes only four-wheel-drive vehicles with chains, can get through. It is no accident that town meeting is timed to come just before the roads unlock. I myself live on a paved road, but I love dirt roads, and every year I can count on getting stuck twice: once in March, because I think my truck will do more than it can; once in May, because I can't believe abandoned roads in the woods aren't dried out yet.

Rivers unlock next. The two I know best, the Connecticut and the Ompom-panoosuc (called the Pompy by those who live along it) both start the same way. You first see two small streams running on top of the ice, one near each frozen bank. Then one day toward the middle of March, a patch of open water appears. Then another. On the Connecticut, which has many dams and much slow water, these patches slowly enlarge for a week, until one day you notice an open channel with a line of ice floes sailing solemnly down the middle.

The Pompy is more dramatic. The whole lower stretch usually opens in a single day. Drive along Vt. Highway 132 the morning of that day. The wind-ing road follows the bends of an ice-locked river with just two or three open pools. Suddenly you notice that at the downstream end of one of those pools there is a little ice jam—half a dozen floes tipped up and piled on each other. These are partially blocking the current and building up pressure. The river has made itself a key.

Come back in two hours, and the jam is now very much bigger and half a mile lower. A surprisingly neat channel stretches away behind it. Even as you watch, the solid ice in front of the jam buckles and breaks, and the whole jam surges ahead. Another twenty feet of river is unlocked. Two more hours, and the Pompy has smashed and broken itself a channel right down to where it flows into the Connecticut. A whole flotilla of ice floes rides out into the bigger river and begins the silent trip south. A few more days, and the Dartmouth crews will be out practicing on the Connecticut, their eight-oared shells dodging the occasional twenty-foot piece of ice that still comes sailing down from Brad-ford. The river is not muddy, and not very high: white-water time is yet to come.

Meanwhile two other kinds of unlocking have been taking place. Town meet-ing marks the resumption of social life. It never wholly ceased during the winter, but, between the cold and the darkness, it slowed down considerably. Now, at what is the real beginning of the year, most of the town gathers to plan the year's business.

Scale is everything. If the million or so voters in Chicago were to gather in one place, you would have at worst a mob and at best a mass audience for leaders to manipulate. But when the eighty or so voters in West Fairlee, Ver-mont, or the several hundred in Thetford gather, you have what feels remark-ably like a true operation of democracy.

I felt this most intensely at Thetford town meeting a few years ago. We met as usual in the high school gymnasium, at 10 A.M. on the first Tuesday after the first Monday in March. The three selectmen, the town clerk, and the moderator of town meeting (he gets $10 a year) were up front. The rest of us—about a hundred and fifty that year—were in folding chairs on the basketball court. Several women from Post Mills, the village whose turn it was to provide lunch that year, were in the back heating casseroles and cutting up pies, occupations that didn't keep them out of either the discussion or the voting.

We had seventeen articles to vote on, all previously announced in the Town Warning. Most of them were pretty small potatoes, such as Article 8: "To see if the Town will appropriate a sum of money, not to exceed $200.00, for Thetford Volunteer Fire Department." (We did.) But Article 12 was the biggest potato in four or five years. It concerned the covered bridge in Thetford Center, one of the two left in town. (There were once six. Two perished of neglect long ago; two were dismantled by the Army Engineers when they built a flood control dam in 1952. It's to control floods in Hartford, Connecticut, not Thetford.)

The Thetford Center bridge was too small for big trucks to go through. It was also badly in need of repair. The selectmen and the one businessman in town who operates big trucks wanted to tear it down and put up a modern concrete highway bridge. Most people thought they would succeed.

We got through the first eleven articles in less than an hour. Then we spent the rest of the morning arguing—"debating" is too elevated a term for town meeting style—Article 12. Sentiment gradually mounted for keeping the covered bridge, chiefly because of the brilliant fight put up by an old man who had been our rural mail carrier for fifty-one years—had taken the mail through that bridge in a horse and sleigh, then a 1911 Cadillac, and finally a Jeep station wagon. It came near time to vote. Then one of the proponents of the new concrete bridge got up, holding a formidable list in his hand. He is a leader in town. He told us he liked the old wooden bridge as well as anyone—but he wasn't sure we realized how much it would cost to repair it. And he began reading specifications and prices from his list: the number of new 12″ × 12″ bridge timbers required, and what each would cost; numbers and prices for joists, and so on. The total kept mounting; we taxpayers began having second thoughts.

Then a young fellow in back stood up, a workingman with a lumberjack's shirt on and a three-day growth of beard. "I don't know where he got them prices from," he said, "but I know this. I work up to the mill in Ely, and we can sell you all that stuff a hell of a lot cheaper than what he said." Every head turned to stare. Undeterred, he went from memory through each item the other man had mentioned, repeating the figures and then quoting the lower price his mill could offer.

After that we voted. Usually we have voice votes to save time, but this was an important decision, and the selectmen passed out slips of paper. We wrote "Yes" if we wanted a new bridge, "No" if we didn't. We filed by the ballot box and dropped the slips in, and when we finished the selectmen counted them. It took fifteen minutes. The First Selectman then walked to the microphone. "Guess we're keepin' it," he said. "Twenty-one 'Yes,' hundred and twenty-one 'No.'" There was a brief roar of triumph. Then we had lunch.

The other March unlocking is done with a brace and bit, and it consists of tapping the maples. But unlocking, alias mud time, alias sugar season, continues from March into April, and I shall save it for then.

April

You know how it is with an April day
When the sun is out and the wind is still,
You're one month on in the middle of May.
But if you so much as dare to speak,
A cloud comes over the sunlit arch,
A wind comes off a frozen peak,
And you're two months back in the middle of March.
          —Robert Frost, "Two Tramps in Mud Time"

The Vermont character is more formed in April than at any other time of year. By "the Vermont character" I mean a combination of wariness, stoicism, and unruffled acceptance of things as they happen that is quite different from the usual American character. You might say that most Americans believe that all problems are in the end soluble, while most Vermonters know better. Naturally weather has a lot to do with why.

In cities—in New York, for example—any intrusion of the weather is regarded as a kind of affront. If it rains at 5 P.M., people don't actually hold the mayor responsible, but they do stand under their umbrellas waiting for taxis in some indignation. Their shoes were not designed for rain; why has someone not put a dome over the city?

If it rains very hard and there is flooding; if, say, the Sixth Avenue subway is delayed by water on the tracks, people do indeed hold the city responsible. Delays are unnatural and intolerable. A cure must be found, just as summer has been cured by air conditioning, and mud season by paving most of the city.

There is no cure for Vermont weather. It is consistent only in its inconsistency. (Once during a drought there was a half-hour's hard rain on the back part of my farm; not a drop fell on the house and garden.) April is the most inconsistent of all. If anything, Frost understates the case. Here is a sequence, for example, from April 1967, at a time when I was keeping unusually close track of the weather:

April 3: So hot in the morning that my small daughters were out playing bare to the waist, and day lily shoots appeared. It turned abruptly cold at 3 P.M., and there were gusts of snow. April 4: Twenty-four above at breakfast time. Cold and sunny all day. April 5: Almost hot. Under a powerful sun, nearly all remaining snow-drifts melted from fields. April 6: Mild, cloudy . . . and snowing. Two inches of snow fell, and stuck. The result was a very beautiful afternoon. All small ponds had melted and were open water, now surrounded by, and reflecting, snow-covered grass and bushes. April 7: Rain and sleet from dawn until 9 A.M.—the roads glazed with ice—driving terrible. It then turned to snow, and five inches of wet flakes came pelting down. Trees worse bent than any time this winter. If I weren't so worried about losing a lot of them, I would think their poses beautiful. April 8: Sunny and warm. The trees erect again by noon, but the fields remain snow-covered.

There is no rational way to deal with a stretch of weather like this. If you wake up to an April snow, you have to go on and shovel—and the town has to plow a hundred miles or so of roads—even though you know perfectly well that by noon it may be a hot day and the snow will melt by itself. Right now it's 7 A.M., and people have to get to work. Besides, it may equally well turn cold and snow twice as hard in the afternoon. Optimists lose every time in a Vermont April.

This is not to say there are no pleasures in the month. On the contrary, starting about April 10, there is an endless series of them, as unlocking turns to spring. First the pussy willows come out, and the rivers run emerald green. Then the deer come out. Mid-April is the best time of the whole year for watching deer. After a winter of eating nothing but tree buds, and not too many of them, they are mad for grass. They come boldly into the fields to eat last year's withered stems. One morning this past April I saw fourteen in the pasture behind my house.

A few days later the robins arrive, sometimes in flocks of two or three hundred, brightening the bare brown southern hillsides. About the same time, spring peepers start up. Then fields begin to green. For some reason, the green always appears first where the snow has melted last. Roughly one day after the first green tips appear, the first woodchuck pops up. Woodchucks are great gourmets, and they are not about to eat old winter-killed hay, as the deer do. In the April sun their brown fur has red glints to it; for a couple of weeks, until the grass gets long or a neighbor boy appears with a .22, they make nice accent marks in the fields.

But the greatest April pleasure is sugaring. It is as common as movies in Chicago. Back in Dr. Williams' time, two-thirds of the families in the state (his estimate) spent part of the month gathering sap and boiling. Fifty years later another Vermont clergyman could write proudly (and truthfully), "Next to Louisiana, the state of Vermont is the greatest sugar-producing state in the Union." Even now you seldom meet a native Vermonter who has not at some time in his life worked in a sugarhouse.

Sugaring usually begins in mid-March and runs until mid-April. These dates are anything but fixed, however, Vermont weather being what it is. This past spring the first good run in Thetford didn't come until March 29th, and most of us closed down around April 23. A few diehards kept boiling until the first of May.

One joy of sugaring is that you take advantage of the inconstant weather. In fact, the more capricious the weather, the more spring seems to come and then dances away again, the better the sugaring. You can't do it at all without freezing nights and warm days, which is why the English attempt to set up a maple industry in England in the eighteenth century failed. An English spring is too equable. But it goes further than that. A late wet April snow is simply frustrating for a motorist, or a suburbanite impatient to get to work on his lawn. For a syrup maker it is cause for rejoicing, because maples run their fastest on such a day. Most of the season you do well to get three or four inches of sap in the bottom of each bucket over a twenty-four-hour period, but on the day of a sugar snow, your best buckets fill to the brim and run over. That night you boil until midnight, and there is a holiday atmosphere.

Human beings are not the only creatures who love sugar season. As soon as the first bugs of the year hatch out, they fly unerringly to the nearest sap bucket and gorge. A moth can't drink much, though, and I don't begrudge him his drop or two. I don't even mind the occasional field mouse who makes his way into the sugarhouse and, holding onto the top of the pan with his hind feet, leans way down and drinks half a teaspoonful of partly boiled syrup. But this past spring I had a more formidable rival, a small brown horse named Dr. Pepper. Dr. Pepper, who belonged to my two daughters, wintered in a newly fenced pasture across the road from the house. It has a nice thirty-bucket grove of maples at the upper end, on which I happened to hang my first thirty buckets. For the first several days I got no sap at all, and I thought I simply must have forgotten that they were late trees. Then about the fourth day I noticed half a dozen horse hairs in the first bucket I checked—and then spotted what I should have earlier: that Dr. Pepper had a well-defined path going to every bucket.

I changed all the lids from the hinged kind, which he could (and did) tip up, to the flanged kind that you have to slide off. He instantly learned to do this with his teeth. In the end I had to put him in with the beef cattle (I was reluctant to, because he bullies them and takes their hay), but not before losing a hundred gallons or so of sap. Woodchucks, I am happy to say, are too short to reach the buckets.

When sugar season ends, spring has arrived. The maples are budding, which is what makes it end in the first place; the skunk cabbage is out; and fields are completely green. There is still a little mound of snow on the north side of the barn, and there are rims of ice on shady coves in the river. But the incredible luxuriance of our late spring has already begun. Everything but the granite has put out shoots, and even that is likely to have patches of bright green moss.

I am speaking, naturally, of most years. Vermont being Vermont, there is an occasional April when everything stays locked in right through the month. I have not myself lived through such an April, but I have heard about several, and I have read Hosea Beckley's *History of Vermont,* published in 1846. He has much to say about the winter of 1842. That year in April they were three months back, in the middle of January. In his own words: "The snow was four feet deep in Brattleboro, the first week in April; and in the mountain towns, from five to seven. The sleighing continued about six months."

May

May 19th, 1838. At home all day. Fine weather. Three hands clearing on hill. Ploughing on meaddows. James Beatie was here. He says he has been to Washington [Vt.]. He passed Cabbot mountain. He said the snow was 3 inches deep. . . . Planted the potatoes and sowed the garden seeds. May 22d. At home. Fine weather. All well. The Canada plum trees are blown out.

—The diary of Henry Stevens of Vermont

Spring lasts exactly one month in Vermont. The whole season gets crammed into May. It's hard to say which is busier, plants or people. May is the month for setting out trees, spreading manure, plowing gardens, buying livestock, cleaning up farms. (By June the long grass will hide just about any object smaller than a tractor.) It is also the month when everything that knows how to blossom does blossom, and everything else grows a foot longer. As there are occasional sharp frosts throughout the month, and not only on Cabot Mountain, men and plants both have to be gamblers.

One sight, one smell, and one sound dominate the first half of May. The sight is the lovely fresh green of new grass and new leaves, punctuated at intervals by the blossoms of the serviceberry, by far the earliest tree in Vermont to flower. It will have edible berries in June. I am told the Indians used to use them for making pemmican; on my farm the birds harvest them so fast I have hardly ever seen a ripe one.

The smell, overwhelming to city nostrils because so organic, is that of the winter manure pile, now dispersed over the fields. I once had a class of college students out about the tenth of May, on a particularly warm, still, high-humidity evening. One boy from Philadelphia kept snuffing the rich air with a worried expression. Finally he said, "Sir, we're not going to get some kind of terrible disease, are we?" I assured him his worst danger was that he might put out leaves.

As for the sound, it's running water. The last snow is going, or has just gone, in the woods. There is still plenty on the mountains. Every stream is running high and cold, and roaring when it comes to a fall or a rapids. That's frequently. Especially in the villages, because most settlements in Vermont were made where there was water power to run a mill or two. Right below the covered bridge in Thetford Center, for example, the Pompy drops fifty feet in a series of rapids and small falls. There are the ruins of four or five old mills on the banks, and right next to the bridge there is a comparatively new dam. A farmer named Charles Vaughan built it in 1916 and introduced electricity to Thetford. (The lights went off at eleven every night, because Mr. Vaughan shut down his turbine and went to bed.)

When the Army engineers took control of the lower Pompy in 1948, Mr. Vaughan broke a notch in the middle of his dam before shutting down the turbine for good, and the river goes through that notch still. Most of the year it runs about halfway up the notch. After a heavy rain, or in a month like April, it runs up to the top. But now the Pompy is pouring sheetlike over the entire dam, and its solemn roar is audible throughout the village. It is not quite so impressive as the Stevens River in Barnet, which comes down a cliff and under the main highway, sending (in May) a cloud of mist over half the village and a roar over half the valley, but it will do.

Along about the middle of May spring visibly shifts gear. It goes into high. For plants, this means something new coming into flower or leaf almost every day. For men it means mowing the lawn three times a week, and a rush to get everything transplanted you're going to transplant. For example, a thousand red pines from the state nursery, or a dozen maples from the woods. There are said to be men who can plant 400 pine seedlings a day, working alone. I find that I collapse after 250.

Some of the changes occurring now are comparatively gradual, like the first apple trees coming into blossom a branch at a time, or the lilacs working up for two weeks from bud to flower. Some happen overnight, or seem to. One day there is not a dandelion in sight; the next there is a river of them flowing down the swale in one's pasture. They look so bounteous and so clear a yellow that I have overcome my childhood suburban prejudice and am now almost as fond of dandelions as sheep are. (My daughter Margaret's one-time wether, Francis, went through the May of his lambhood eating as many as five hundred or a thousand dandelions daily. He survived to become a notably large sheep.) One day there is nothing to wild strawberries except a few pleasant memories from last year; the next, there are blossoms wherever the meadow grass is poor and thin enough to give them any sun. That means several million blossoms on almost every farm.

Late May is when the gambling occurs. Frost-hating trees are unable to resist the sun any longer, and put out their leaves. The oaks, for example, do.

Every few years a really hard frost comes to punish them. There was such a frost on May 22, 1969, but I had forgotten about it when on the twenty-eighth I noticed that every leaf on every oak on the place had turned black. The maples, the birches, the mountain ash, and every other tree looked fine: I concluded that some new blight must have struck. I cautiously asked a neighbor how his oaks were doing. He looked surprised. "That frost got them, if that's what you mean," he said. A week later each oak had tiny new leaves. They keep a spare set of buds.

Frost-fearing men are able to resist planting their gardens until Memorial Day, but the rest of us get overwhelmed by a desire to beat the weeds. Peas and lettuce don't matter; they laugh at frost. Corn and tomatoes are more delicate. Since corn takes about ten days to come up, men guess when the last frost could possibly be (it usually comes at full moon), and plant nine days earlier. As for tomatoes, one of the commonest sights in the state is everyone rushing out to the tomato bed on a cold evening with blankets and bushel baskets and sap buckets. But we also keep a spare set of seeds.

That's the wrong note to end on, however. May is not a cautious or a suffering month in Vermont, it's expansive and triumphant. For me its symbol is a certain crab apple tree in the old school district of Rice's Mills, two miles from Thetford Center. (Legally, Rice's Mills is an undifferentiated part of the town of Thetford. The name no longer applies to a school and never was a postal address—it's just a memory. But we all use it.)

This is a particularly large and vigorous crab apple, standing near the base of a southern slope. Its crown of pink blossoms must be thirty feet across. At noon on a sunny day it is a temple of the bees. Portly bumblebees, wasps, hornets, honeybees form a joyful cloud around it and in it. You can hear the many-noted hum before you are near enough to see the largest bee. I think of that scene—the pink sunlit tree, the moving cloud of bees, the hum like a dynamo—as being the closest I'll ever get to Mother Nature personified. That hum and the roar of the Pompy are the two voices of spring. The Pompy's is pure power. The tree's is pure fecundity.

June

Now I return to the Spot where I used to toil and tup at the hoe, &
when I meet them [old friends] I feel as though it would be the
happy-fying of my days to return and live with them, but the idea of
working for a living would dispell all idear of living in Vermont.
—The journal of James Guild, late of Tunbridge, Vermont, 1824

Guild was right on both counts. It is the happyfying of one's days to be in
Vermont in June—and if one is a farmer, it is too much work. June is hay
time. The average farmer has about fifty tons to mow, rake, bale or gather
loose, and get to the barn.

I have tried it both ways. I have hayed with one neighbor who has a pair of
workhorses, a horse-drawn loader, a big old blue-painted hay wagon, and a
plentiful supply of pitchforks. I have done it with another who has a tractor so
big that he can pull a baler and a wagon simultaneously. The baler automatically
flips the bales into the wagon. Still, one must stack them as they come, and
they come fast. It is just as hard and hot work as building a load with a pitch-
fork, though less interesting.

A farmer's whole year is too much work. Milking twice a day (practically all
Vermont farmers are dairy farmers) 365 days a year, holidays and one's birth-
day not excepted, is hard work. So is dealing with all that manure. A farmer is
endlessly repairing machinery, reroofing barns, fixing fence, laying pipeline, doc-
toring cattle. Nearly everything that most people call someone else in to do he
does for himself, or he couldn't afford to stay in business. It's toil and tup.
Which is one reason that there were 36,000 farms in Vermont in Guild's time,
and the official count now is 6874. A lot of farmers have decided to cut their
work week down from a hundred hours to forty, and they have taken cushy
jobs as loggers, or driving trailer trucks, or maybe they have left Vermont and
work at Pratt & Whitney in Connecticut.

At the same time, because you *do* do forty or fifty different kinds of work
in a month, farming is the most continuously interesting occupation I know.
Old-fashioned farming, that is. Being in an enclosed, air-conditioned super-
tractor, ploughing a flat thousand-acre wheat farm in Manitoba must not be
all that different from driving a trailer truck. But behind the horses in Norwich,

Vermont, or on the open tractor in Thetford, mowing up hill and down, one sees the Indian paintbrush come out in early June, and the black-eyed Susans in the middle. One stops and picks a handful of wild strawberries. A rainy day comes, and one shifts to cutting fence posts, or maybe packaging the last of the syrup.

The solution, of course, is to be a part-time farmer. Many people have found it. Those 29,000 farms that have vanished since Guild's time have by no means all gone back to woods, or turned into summer places, or been developed by Boise Cascade. Most of them are farms still, but part-time farms, and hence not counted by the Department of Agriculture. A man quits milking, sells his herd and his bulk tank, gets a job in town. But he keeps a few head of beef cattle, and he keeps sugaring. Or a man moves to Vermont (and not always a man, either—I know a girl in St. Johnsbury who's done it), supports himself with a teaching job or a craft, and then buys an old farm to occupy his weekends. Two years later he has learned how to lay stone wall and use a chain saw, and he has just gotten his first check for the sale of fleeces from his thirty sheep.

Farming is a poor way to make a living, because you have to go into factory farming to make it pay. It is the best hobby there is—and, in fact, "hobby" is too little a word. The best way of life. Not just because you learn forty different trades, and not just because you follow the seasons, but because you get to spend your whole life producing a single work of art. That is, the farm itself. You thin a hedgerow here, improve a woodlot there, make a pond across the road. You prune up the old apple trees, and simultaneously make your orchard more beautiful and begin to get good apples again. You keep the beef cattle partly to get the beef, but partly because the six-acre pasture looks better when it's grazed. (Envy of how it looks was what led to suburban lawns in the first place.)

Some people make their own bodies a lifetime work of art. It's too small a surface to be worthy of that much attention; and, anyway, for the last thirty or even forty years of the owner's life it's a work of art whose aesthetics steadily diminish. Depressing. Some make their houses and apartments lifetime or long-time works of art. The house at least endures. But again there is not enough scope. When it's all furnished and remodeled and ornamented, there is nothing much left but dusting, and polishing the windows. A farm, on the other hand, can keep on changing and getting more beautiful for a thousand years. Maples that I don't even know who planted, back in 1840, line my hay lane. They make a leafy tunnel from which one emerges into the sunlit field. The ones I myself plant across the road I will live to see as tall young trees. A century from now, if a developer doesn't get hold of the place, they will have become one of the best parts of the view from the farmhouse windows. Not to mention a fine addition to the sugar potential.

A part-time farmer, who can take a June afternoon off to go swimming, who can afford to judge aesthetics equally with profit (as somehow the men who farmed here a hundred and fifty years ago seemed to), he is happyfied indeed. And when he spends a long June day mowing and raking, he is not only getting hay for the winter; he is in effect giving the face of his farm its annual shave, and he is drunk with delight at how well it looks.

July

The cupidity of a few land-jobbers . . . gave rise to Vermont as a separate, independent jurisdiction.
            —The Rev. Hosea Beckley, *History of Vermont,* 1846

To specify each locality in Vermont possessing attractions to the summer tourist, or inducements to one wishing to build a summer home, would require nearly a complete description of each town.
            —*Resources and Attractions of Vermont, with a List of Desirable Homes for Sale.* State Board of Agriculture, 1892

There are said to be 250,000 [milk] cows in the state, which under normal conditions bring in an income of about $22 million a year. Now if 250,000 summer guests could be accommodated . . . it would bring an income into the state of $25 million.
            —*Rural Vermont: A Program for the Future.* By Two Hundred Vermonters, 1931

July is heralded in Vermont by tiger lilies, by the ripening of wild raspberries (the middle link in the summer-long chain of wild strawberries, raspberries, and blackberries), and by the arrival of the summer people. June was summer (and summer people), too, with plenty of days in the seventies and eighties, and many city dwellers to enjoy them. July is high summer. It is a relatively quiet time for the landscape—the exuberance of spring is long gone. Pines and spruces, which in late May were getting three inches taller a week, now merely deepen their color. Grass can be mowed once a week. Roaring Branch in Arlington whispers over its rocks; the Mad River in Waitsfield and Wild Brook in North Walcott are tamed. My daughters swim where two months ago the Pompy shot through a gorge at twenty miles an hour (or what seemed like it, anyway). Vermont is a settled and permanent green. It is almost impossible to believe that winter ever existed, much less will come again.

Only one thing grows wildly in July, and that's the population. All over the state, motels and campgrounds do a peak business. Summer houses are all open.

Despite the heat, and July is the one month with much unpleasantly hot weather, carpenters are working busily building new ones, usually not a bit like the white clapboard and brick and stone houses already here. Black-toppers are paving driveways into what six months ago were upland pastures and orchards. The highways are crowded (by local standards) with moving vans, U-Haul trucks, and shiny new mobile homes.

For about a hundred years Vermonters sought this growth. They cultivated out-of-staters as they would any other crop. The visitors, for their part, were mostly content to ripen quietly in their assigned fields—that is, the summer hotels in places like Manchester and Woodstock, the special summer-people villages like Thetford Hill. Or sometimes they would board with a farm family. Any of these ways they contributed nicely to the revenue but didn't much interfere with the landscape.

This has now changed, with, on the whole, dire consequences. Now the visitors want the land. It's worse than a rebellion of the cows would be.

Up until about ten years ago land in Vermont had a value directly based on its productivity. Good farmland might cost you as much as $100 an acre; rocky hillside went for $10. Summer-people land, of course, went for a lot more, but that was mostly limited to a narrow strip around each lake and around certain villages. Elsewhere, you could buy a hundred acres knowing that if you chose to work it, the land would yield enough to pay the taxes and a modest return besides. If you didn't, you restored forest and deer.

Now the value of land throughout the state is based on its potential for development. If your field could be a subdivision with not too much expense for putting the roads through, it is suddenly worth $1000 or $2000 an acre, and you are taxed on that basis. Even though as working land it earns no more than it did ten years ago. Even though all you want to do is keep Holsteins on it and raise cucumbers. A Vermont farm has come to be like a speculative stock, which pays an annual dividend of twenty cents a share but is priced at $85. With this difference: that the stock speculator pays no tax until and if he sells, but the farmer may face an annual tax bill larger than his whole income from his farm. Only the very rich (which as many as two Vermont farmers are) can afford the taxes on much development land. And there is now no other kind.

The state is perfectly aware of this problem and has passed a law providing that anyone in the state may deed his development rights to one of several state agencies, such as the Fish and Game Department. (It, of course, would not exercise them—couldn't; it doesn't own the land.) Since most of the cash value of a Vermont farm lies in the possibility of cutting it up into half-acre lots, the assessment would promptly plummet, and the farmer could once again afford his taxes. The only problem is that as the state has not as yet appropriated a penny to implement the bill, the state agencies adamantly refuse to be given any development rights.

Meanwhile, the transfer of land moves steadily forward from native farmers to out-of-state land-investment firms and a few instate ones. And from them, in small parcels, to people who want to summer in Colonial Village, formerly the Perkins place. One of the commonest July sights is the auction notice at the village store, beginning "As I have discontinued farming. . . ."

All is not lost. Part-time farmers, when they can afford it, are buying a good deal of the land. An occasional man who can't bear to see a two-hundred-year-old work of art bulldozed deeds his farm entire to the town or the state. We have such a one in Thetford. And nature is not wholly idle. Even as developers move into Vermont from the southeast, coyotes are moving in from the northwest. We may strike a new balance yet.

There are twenty-three broad views of Vermont pictured in this book, not one of them containing either a human being or a vehicle. (In two you can see tire tracks where a car has been.) The pictures were taken with no cheating, no waiting for a lull in the traffic. Even in July there are still hundreds of places where you can sit all day and see no summer person, no native, no camper truck, no motel, no Burger Boy. Only the otter in the river, the foal by the barn. In twenty years?

August

We have no populous towns, seaports, or large manufactories, to collect the people together. They are spread over the whole country, forming small and separate settlements.

—Samuel Williams, 1794

I don't even know how many separate settlements there are in Vermont. There are 238 *towns,* plus our eight cities. Subtract the 100,000 people who live in the cities from the 450,000 in the state, and that leaves an average of 1500 people per town. (Nearer 3000 in August.) Reasonably small, yes.

But a New England town is like a Midwestern township. It is a unit of government, it covers thirty-six square miles, and it has nothing much to do with where people actually live. In the town of Thetford, for example, there are either five and a half or six settlements, depending on how you count. East Thetford and North Thetford are river villages, two miles apart, on the bank of the Connecticut. I would guess each has a couple of hundred people. Each has a post office, a filling station, and a store. East Thetford also has a sawmill and a good restaurant; North Thetford has a toy-maker, a stone hotel, and a Congregational church. One of the very few in the country, I am told, with a gold pineapple on top of the steeple.

Thetford Hill sits on top of the first high ridge you come to when you start west from the river—five hundred feet above East Thetford. It has a stunning view back into New Hampshire, it has the town high school, it has about ninety residents in the winter and at least three hundred in the summer. Also the original (1773) and still biggest church in town, and a post office. No stores.

Go down the other side of the ridge, and in a mile you come to Thetford Center, strung out along the Pompy. Once it had an ax factory and a shutter mill. It still has a post office, a store, one of the best mechanics in the state, the town hall, a beautiful little brick Methodist church, and two hundred people. Also my farm.

Keep going, and in another four miles, just before you reach the western border of the town, there's another rapid on the Pompy, and the village of Post Mills. It was formerly the site of a fishing-rod factory. Currently it's dominated by a mill that makes blanks for chair legs out of rock maple and yellow birch logs, though it also has two rival general stores and a markedly rural airport. I still haven't mentioned Union Village, which is half in Thetford and half in Norwich—hence the name—or Sawney Bean, a sort of half-community up in the highest valley in town.

In August most of these settlements are busy celebrating their separateness. Thetford Hill has a fair the first week in August, a very elegant and wonderful fair. Union Village puts on two church suppers during the month—I always try to get to them both—and North Thetford celebrates with an all-day fete and auction. In the Center we had our fair, called Old Home Day, back in July.

Over the whole state there must be hundreds of such suppers and fetes and fairs. If I had time and appetite, I think I would go to them all. I *have* been to a good many. Ranging from the heartrendingly small, like the sugar-on-snow supper held each April in the basement of the two-room schoolhouse in Vershire, to the large and bustling, like Norwich Fair. That has ox-pulling contests, and a Ferris wheel, and last year to please my daughters I made the bell ring six times in the strong-man contest, and won them each a stuffed animal. (After that I collapsed in the shade, while they went for a ride in a Stanley Steamer.)

One reason for going to suppers and fairs is simply that it gives you a chance to see the villages they're held in. There are almost no beautiful cities in America, though there are beautiful parts of cities, and some sections that are glorious without being beautiful, like downtown Chicago. Cities are too big and too rich for beauty; they have outgrown themselves too many times. Seen from a distance, so that they seem little again, like New York viewed from the harbor, or almost any city perceived as a jewel-pattern of lights when you fly over it at night, they are indeed beautiful, but that's another matter.

A settlement of two hundred people, on the other hand, has never outgrown itself. It has no sections; it's all one piece. If most of its houses were built in the late eighteenth and early nineteenth centuries, and if the whole village is set in green hills, it stands an excellent chance of being beautiful. Most villages in Vermont are.

Another reason to go, of course, is the food. Different settlements pride themselves on different specialties. Union Village is very strong on chicken pie. Thetford Center is famous—in a ten-mile radius—for red flannel hash. In Fairlee they import lobsters. If you work at the supper, as opposed to just going, or if you have a friend in the kitchen, you can even help support your farm. The first year I kept pigs, my little boar and sow lived throughout August and well into September on a stunningly good diet of scrapings—homemade piecrust left on plates by people who don't eat the crust even of pie made by the best cook in Sawney Bean, and so on. A good supper will yield you forty pounds.

Even apart from the fairs, August is a wonderful month. The corn, the tomatoes, the baby carrots, the little cowhorn potatoes are finally ready to eat. It is still high summer and good for swimming, but there is often a week of weather at a time when it's cool enough morning and evening to need a fire in the wood-stove. Sometime about the middle of the month, the morning mists begin. Each day when they clear you get the kind of weather that can only be described as blessed. All colors and shapes are unusually distinct, even the corners of shadows seem extra sharp, and even in hot sun there is the faintest hint of chill. Yet you are not cold.

Best of all is when such a mist comes on in the late evening instead of at dawn, and one is awake to see it arrive. There is a two-hundred-foot hill behind my sugarhouse, once grazed by cattle and still clear on top. The night of August 24, 1970, my wife and I climbed it at midnight by bright moonlight. Five minutes after we reached the top, a puff of mist came around the valley wall, heading upriver from Union Village. In half an hour we were on a moonlit island above a valley full of mist. By one o'clock the mist had lapped up over the hilltop, and we had watched our view shorten from seven miles (the hills beyond Post Mills) to a hundred feet. We had seen the nearest treeline fade and become ghostly, and then vanish, and finally we started down in a faintly luminous white cloud. We got very wet.

Such nights are exceptional. Any day in August is good for driving to a village or two, though. Villages are the glory of the state, as the American painter Charles Eldridge realized a long time ago. Eldridge, an extremely urban young man from Hartford, Connecticut (itself more urban in those pre-Los Angeles days than it seems now), paid a visit to Vermont in 1833. He was going to Montpelier on the stagecoach. Since he knew it to be the state capital, he figured it must be something like Hartford. It wasn't. Still isn't. The population has yet to reach 10,000 and was about 3700 then. Not many monumental buildings, either. "We were disappointed in the view," Eldridge wrote, "and felt a little chagrin, that in point of size and elegance, we had expected too much of Montpelier." Then he stopped to consider why. "But in fact there had been in our route, many villages too beautiful to have a superior even in the principal town."

September

It would have been a pleasure to bring Rubio to Thetford in September and watch him eat his words. Better weather doesn't occur. The occasional mists of August are now a regular thing, with the result that every morning the sun rises with power enough to send the dew steaming up from roofs—and then the valleys fill with light cloud, and the sunlight slowly fades. The morning stays fresh and cool for about four hours. Then the sun burns through again, and a clear day follows, crisp and golden.

All creatures respond to the winy air. If you call your two Hereford cattle for their daily quart of grain, they come at the first shout (in July they didn't even look up until the third), and they come at a rocking bovine canter, out of pure high spirits. Sedentary men are to be found climbing mountains. Even a house cat will sometimes charge across the lawn and let his momentum take him ten feet up a maple, just to show how good he feels. It is ideal harvest weather. There is finally plenty of corn. If it weren't for the frost that's looming ahead now, certain to kill the garden, and if it weren't for the yellow leaves that begin to appear as warnings on birches and elms, Vermonters might forget in September that they are not supposed to be optimists.

Not only the weather is smiling. One of the delights of a farm is that a dozen times a year you have a profusion of something—more watermelons or blueberries or walnuts than you can possibly use. You possess an innocent and prodigal wealth. It is the opposite remove from the little pinched economies of supermarket buying—the four tomatoes in a cellophane package, the single cantaloupe for forty-nine cents. (I was going to say the single pumpkin for a dollar fifty, until I realized that most supermarkets don't even *have* pumpkins. They sell objects made of orange plastic.)

Vermont is no cornucopia as farmland goes, but we have our times of profusion, too, and the greatest of them comes in September. Apples. There's hardly a farm in the state that doesn't have apple trees along half the fence-lines, and an old apple orchard besides. Even in deep woods you constantly come on old apple trees still bearing away—half-forgotten species like Pound Sweets and Greenings.

There is a fine, careless freedom in walking through the orchard the first week in September, testing an apple from each tree to see if it's ripe—taking one bite and then tossing it away. No harm in that; it will go back to humus.

Not that it always gets a chance, this early in the season. Deer adore apples, and a few hours later you are likely to see a young doe approach the orchard at a brisk trot. She circles the first tree, she finds and eats your bitten apple and the one windfall that has come down since her last visit. Then she trots to the next tree. If not enough apples are down, sometimes she will stand on her hind legs and begin picking from the lower branches. September is the second-best time of year for watching deer.

By the middle of the month most apples *are* ripe. (Duchesses were ripe in August, and people were busy making pink applesauce.) Now is Vermont like a Brueghel painting. Men with their own barrels are gathered at the cider mills, laying in a winter's supply. The smaller commercial orchards, these days run mostly on a pick-your-own basis, swarm with people and pickup trucks and bushel baskets. Every small child has an apple in one hand that he is eating, and an apple in the other hand that he (now) thinks he is going to eat immediately afterward.

Some of the part-time farmers are fortunate enough to have one of the home cider presses that Sears Roebuck sold by the thousand at the turn of the century—and doesn't bother to stock at all now, alas. They consist of a hand-turned grinder and a press with a capacity of one bushel, all mounted as one neat unit. A few people are still more fortunate and also have an old nineteenth-century chopper—one or two part-time blacksmiths in Vermont have started making them again—and its accompanying wooden bowl.

On a particularly golden Sunday afternoon last September, I was one of a dozen people gathered at such a farm. Most of us had glass or plastic cider jugs we had brought with us. On this particular place it is the wife who does most of the part-time farming, and she had a light wagon hitched to her driving mare, Chiquita, so that we could all move through the orchard tossing apples into one container. In half an hour we gathered a dozen bushels, not worrying in the least about bruises or rust, because these apples were about to become cider. Not worrying about pesticides, either, because this orchard is unsprayed.

Then for a couple of hours we took turns chopping apples in the great wooden bowl, running them through the grinder (one to turn the handle and one to keep feeding chunks of apple in) and pressing them. We wound up with ten gallons of cider, a lot of unused apples, and about a hundred pounds of pomace, which is what is left after you grind apples and press them.

Pomace is to horses as Granola is to teen-agers, and most of this went to our hostess's work team. But one basketful I brought home to my pigs. Pigs love pomace so much that they got into an ugly fight—easily settled, however, by my shaking down and throwing them a couple of hundred apples from a tree near their pen. Then I walked over to the garden to get some fresh corn for supper. We had almost had a frost the night before—the temperature had dropped to thirty-three—but the mist had arrived just in time to save us, and the corn was unhurt. On the way back I tossed the stalks to the pigs—pigs dote on cornstalks—and I noticed that one maple over on Houghton Hill had overnight turned bright red.

October

All the hills blush; I think that autumn must be the best season to journey over even the Green *Mountains. You frequently exclaim to yourself, what* red *maples!*
— Henry David Thoreau, 1850

A solitary maple on a woodside flames in single scarlet, recalls nothing so much as the daughter of a noble house dressed for a fancy ball, with the whole family gathered round to admire her before she goes.
— Henry James, *The American Scene,* 1907

October belongs to the trees. There is already a good deal of color when the month begins, especially along the roads. In fact, there is considerably more than there was in Thoreau's time or Henry James's. This is not because of any change in the climate, but because of a change in the way we take care of the roads.

When they came tree-looking, every road in the state was dirt, and salt was something you used in making salt pork. Winter road care consisted of packing the snow down with giant rollers, to assure a good sleighing surface.

About fifty years ago rolling went out and plowing came in. It didn't hurt the trees a bit, except occasionally when the plow nicked one. For that matter, it didn't even keep the roads from staying snowy all winter. The layer of snow on top of the dirt was just much thinner (and mud season somewhat shorter). Present-day dirt roads still are white in the winter, which is why they get photographed so much.

The trouble came with paving. That is, quite recently. Ten years ago not only most back roads but some state highways like Vt. 100 and even a couple of far-northern stretches of U. S. 5 were dirt. Now most are paved. A paved road can't have a layer of snow, or else some of it melts and refreezes as ice and everybody skids and has accidents. On with the salt. Handy for cars, maybe necessary for large trucks, but terrible for trees. Their roots pick up the salt in the spring, and they slowly sicken and die.

Meanwhile, they put on a splendid show. A sick tree turns color and sheds its leaves a trifle earlier each year, so that most roadside trees are now two weeks to a month ahead of the rest. On October 1 sugar maples by the road are orange—or already bare—elms are yellow, birches are speckled with lemon color. A brave sight, even though it's the flush of disease.

Away from the roads the landscape is still green. You do see bits of scarlet here and there, which are the sumacs and the red maples. A red maple in the fall is about the reddest thing there is. A strong bold peasant red—noble trees don't rush off to the ball quite so early. You also see some intense yellow where an ash has turned, pulling its usual trick of turning every leaf exactly the same color at exactly the same instant. Bright red and bright yellow. Since the blue skies of September persist and even get bluer in October, hills and sky make a simple pattern of primary colors, with a green background.

As the month progresses, complexity sets in. Trees whose names I don't even know turn a dozen shades of carmine and vermilion and ocher and jonquil. Ferns go bronze; the briers become a deep lustrous maroon. By the time the fall foliage tours arrive in mid-month, every hillside has fifty or so hues to offer. The sugar maple, lord of our trees at any time, rules especially now. A single sugar maple is capable of producing two or three shades of orange, pink, and yellow on just one branch; a grove of them offers such richness of color that the eye can hardly take it in. A four-year-old girl (from New Hampshire, I admit, but just two miles over the border) once gave sugar maples their ultimate praise. She and her mother were collecting leaves in a particularly glowing grove, and when she had about a bushel, all different, she looked up and said thoughtfully, "Mummy, God must spend an awful lot of money on fall."

By late October the fancy-dress ball is over. Oaks in their sensible brown remain, and beeches in gossamer tan, and the evergreens. But all other trees are bare except a few yellow poplars, now going fast. The grass is almost done growing, and in a heavily grazed pasture you are beginning to feed hay. The first killing frost has come. Just exactly when varies not only from year to year but from farm to farm. On mine, which is near but not quite at the bottom of a hill, it has come as late as October 16 (1970) and as early as August 31 (1965). But come it has, and the garden is dead. There is nothing left to harvest but a little late lettuce and the last cider apples. The land is through working for the year.

Men, on the other hand, still have plenty to do. A part-time farmer, indeed, is almost as busy as he was in May, because October is the last month there will be any daylight left when he gets home from work. October days are perhaps the best of the whole year, fresher and cleaner even than those of September, but they are too short. You feel pushed. Provident men are out in the

40

short afternoons cutting next year's wood supply; improvident men are rustling up this year's wood, which they will have to burn green. If you want early peas next spring, you had better prepare the ground now, before it freezes. There are all those storm windows to put up. If you neglected to wash your sap buckets in April, you frantically do it in October. And meanwhile the crisp golden weather tempts you not to work at all. A Saturday when you could perfectly well cut a cord of red maple in the morning, and wash ten storm windows after lunch, and rake a truckload of leaves before dark, you walk up Potato Hill with a sandwich, getting all the views you never got while the leaves were on, picking a few butternuts that the squirrels missed, maybe seeing a fox.

Then one morning at the very end of the month, you go out to feed the pigs, and it's twenty above, and the water in their trough is frozen solid, and you know you must make a last steady drive to get ready before winter comes.

November

Those grace days don't come every year. About one year in two, November starts with rain, moves on to sleet, and by the middle settles in to snow. In 1968, for example, there was a minor blizzard on the thirteenth—bad enough to knock a few trees down across U. S. 5. Then a little more snow on the sixteenth. More still on the seventeenth, and that day my seven-year-old daughter had the first snowmobile ride of her life. (She had been skiing since she was five, though she admittedly started early. They don't teach it in the schools here until second grade.)

As for 1971, a cold ugly rain the morning of the seventh turned into cold beautiful snow that afternoon. We had flurries the next day, and on the ninth it was twelve above. People who still had wood to bring in found it frozen to the ground and were sorry they had not moved faster in October.

But the other half of the years, November is a whole grace month, until locking begins at the very end. Clear skies, pleasant days, and lots of free time. There is always *some* work on a farm, of course. For example, all the pigs that have figured in this book—two nameless pairs, and then a sow and barrow named Bingo and Bacon—went to slaughter in November. I didn't butcher them myself. But merely persuading two large reluctant pigs to get into the back of a pickup truck is a chore. On a sleety morning, as it was with Bingo and Bacon, the chore becomes a nightmare of spinning tires, slippery pigs, and mud-covered people. Loading and delivery took half the morning.

Mostly, though, November time is one's own. The trees are bare: no more leaves to rake. The house is banked, the woodshed full, and you have a fresh-cut cord or two stacked out in the woods. A mild, sunny weekend is a time either to go hunting or exploring. (Or, if you don't have a red shirt and a red hat, a time to stay strictly indoors. Deer season has begun.)

My own choice is to go exploring. Like the rest of rural New England, Vermont is full of ruins where there were once farms. And not only farms, but copper mines and grist mills and little mountain graveyards. Some of these last are still dimly in use. There is one about three miles from my farm that had frequent burials from 1770 to 1900 and has had about one a generation since. It also has one of the prettiest views in the region. Sometime early in the twenty-first century I mean to move down there. I realize I won't get much good of the view, but I still want to be where it is.

There are two ways to go exploring in the country. One is simply to start out in a more or less straight line and see what you come to. You usually just come to woods and more woods, occasionally crossing a dirt road or skirting a still-active farm. The chief pleasure is that now with all the leaves down you can see every old stone wall, where there were once fields and pastures, and you can marvel yet again at the beauty of all that forgotten stonework, and the skill of the makers. You can also see here and there a three-hundred-year-old oak or maple that those early Vermonters spared.

But now and again you find something more. My best November find was up near Five Corners, which sounds heavily settled but isn't. I was going up one of the five roads that make the corners, one no longer passable for cars, and came on a fallen-in house. Usually there's not much to see except a lot of rotten clapboards, and not much to do except fall through the floor yourself and break a leg. This had been a glorious house in its time, though, and even in its decay you could walk cautiously around part of the first floor. Doing so, you came into the living room, and found that it had been plastered so well a hundred and fifty years ago that on two walls the plaster was still sound. And on the plaster some long-ago farmer's wife had painted designs. There were patterns of leaves, and sunbursts, and on either side of the fireplace little groups of prancing horses, three inches high. It seems to me that in museums I see bits of homely Roman mosaic and not very interesting painted Greek vases—neither half so nice to look at as those prancing horses. In the spring I went back with a friend who is an art historian, but the rest of the house had fallen down. We had five feet of snow that winter.

The other way to explore, of course, is with a definite goal in mind. Mine has usually been to find bricks. My farmhouse, when I bought it, had a dirt cellar, as old farmhouses generally do. Little by little I have floored it with eighteenth- and nineteenth-century bricks, most of them found in the woods. Seventeen cellar holes and one copper mine are represented. (This is the same mine that out past the ruin of the smelter has one of the most mysterious and heroic pieces of stonework I have ever seen. I'm not about to say how to get there. It's best stumbled on.)

The charm of old bricks, apart from their being free, lies in their extreme individuality—as bricks go. A good many have finger and thumb prints on one side, from where they were picked up and put in the kiln to be fired. Twice I have found bricks that were dated with the tip of someone's finger. But mostly the brick hunt is an excuse to prowl through the woods with an old town map, locating cellar holes. Once you've found one, you play amateur archaeologist, guessing what sort of house it was, where the barn stood, trying to locate the spring. An armload of rosy old bricks is just a bonus.

The last week of November such games come to an abrupt end. Winter doesn't necessarily begin, but locking does. Sometime within a week on either side of Thanksgiving the ground freezes, not to thaw again until spring. Henceforth any rummaging in cellar holes would have to be done with a pickax. Few animals are to be seen in the woods now. The deer are hiding from the hunters, and most small animals are underground or inside trees until spring. I am ready to be indoors myself.

December

I have cause to remember [Royalton, Vermont] for its wilderness aspect, it abounds with Pine, a thin flashy kind of soil; but what few people inhabit it appear to live tolerable.
    —John Russell Davis, *Diary of a Journey Through Massachusetts, Vermont, and Eastern New York*, 1800

Davis wrote that in June. In December he might have been less sure. December is the bleakest month of the year. No more grace days now. Just cold and darkness, both steadily increasing.

These are drawbacks that Vermont shares with most of the Northern Hemisphere, of course, but both conditions seem especially pronounced here. Vermont is at a higher latitude than people sometimes realize. A man I know left the state a few years ago and moved south. Where he went was Canada. The city of London, Ontario, to be precise, which is a hundred and twenty-five miles south of where he started, in St. Albans, Vermont. If he'd gone to Kingsville, he would have been two hundred miles south, blinking in the sun.

The darkness at least increases in a known and predictable way—and furthermore, by the end of the month the days will have reached their shortest and be growing longer again. The cold is trickier. December begins almost gently. Some years there is snow, and some years there's not. Every year there is gradual locking: little ponds skin over, and then big ones. No lakes yet. Every year dreary cold days alternate with almost as dreary mild ones. There is an overwhelming sense of waiting for something to happen.

Then it happens. With sudden savage force winter begins. The date may be as early as December 5, or as late as the twentieth.

One night you wake up cold and pull up another blanket. No use—you're still cold. In the morning you look at the thermometer and it has dropped to eight below. Yesterday the Pompy and the Connecticut were open water. Today they are ice, except for one smoking patch just below the Ledyard Bridge on the Connecticut, and a few rapids on the Pompy that send gusts of steam fifty feet into the air. A few laboring furnaces break down that night. Several careless newcomers to the state have their first experience with frozen water pipes the next morning. Many cars won't start. From now until spring life is going to be stern.

When you add that by Christmas there is certain to be somewhere between a foot and two feet of snow on the ground, and probably a terrific ice storm, there seems a certain madness in staying here at all. There isn't, though. We not only live tolerable, we live well. Even in bleak December. Some would say especially then. That will remain true as long as the state has its wilderness aspect.

A frozen forest with rivers and lakes in it is a wonderfully accessible place, almost a magical one. There is no magic to a city or a suburban street in cold weather, and not much shelter, either. People simply get to where they're going, the fastest way possible. But a winter forest is a place to go for pleasure.

It's true you had better dress warmly if you plan to be out long; it's also true that the forest itself will shield you. The wind may whistle through city streets, but in woods with any quantity of evergreens (and this state still abounds with Pine, not to mention Tamarack, Spruce, and Cedar), there are innumerable calm glades. In December you can reach them all. The swamps you stayed out of in November you now casually stroll through; a pond is no barrier, but a shortcut. Bring a pair of skates. There are places you can skate ten miles up a river on the new ice and never meet a soul. The trip takes less time than a citizen of Los Angeles needs to drive out to the ice arena, to park, and to get his skates on. The scenery is better, too.

Even nicer is going out on foot with one's children to find a Christmas tree. Bringing a tree home is a pleasure even if you only drive to a shopping center and pay six dollars for one commercially grown. To prowl through your own woods and abandoned fields, considering a tall young pine here and a trim little hemlock there, is delight. Finally you spot a six-foot spruce with especially shapely branches, you let one of the children cut it, and you carry it home in triumph.

Even when heavy snow comes, which it always does before Christmas, the woods are a place to go. Now you set out on skis or by snowmobile, and though the days are short, the sun is bright and the ground so dazzling that it hardly seems men have soiled this planet at all. I admit to thinking occasionally that Southerners have an advantage in that every time they want to step outdoors with their children, they don't have to spend ten minutes struggling with snow-pants and boots and mittens and jackets. But the problem is soluble. A country that can design spaceships is sooner or later going to come up with an efficient winter garment for children—something one-piece from boots to hood that the child zips in or out of in thirty seconds. Then my daughters will come every time to help feed the horses.

46

For some reason it seems nearly always to snow on the last day of the year. It did on New Year's Eve in 1967, again in 1968, again in 1969, again in 1971. About ten inches in 1971. At midnight, as 1972 began, I was at a party in a farmhouse on a hill above a small Vermont village. The snow had almost stopped, and the moon had come out. It was one degree below zero. Almost everyone at the party had come outside to look at the new snow. All around was a silence so total that the world seemed not merely cleansed but newly created. Nowhere was there the sound of a car in that hushed world, or so much as a dog barking. The clear moonlight revealed no mess, either. Men live in Vermont: no doubt there were beer cans and even abandoned refrigerators within easy walk. They were nullified by the snow.

To be outdoors on such a night is to experience that awe which modern man is said to have lost the capacity for, but which he has really just ceased to look for in the right places. To be in the right place is worth almost any price in frozen pipes and jammed snowsuit zippers and dark mornings.

I

2

3

4

5

6

7

9

13

16

17

18–19 ▶

32-33 ▶

34

35

37

40

41

44

45

46–47▶